# SESAME STREET

# Elmo is Red, Cookie is Blue!

by Kathryn Knight

LEVEL  READER

**Pre 1** — READING LEVEL

Published by Dalmatian Press, LLC. All rights reserved.
Printed in Guangzhou, Guangdong, China.

The DALMATIAN PRESS name is a trademark of Dalmatian Publishing Group,
Franklin, Tennessee 37068-2068. 1-866-418-2572.

Elmo is red.

Cookie is blue.

Abby and Elmo say,

"We love you!"

Elmo has one box.

Oscar has a few.

Here a bird.

There a bird.

Now there are two.

Elmo is up.

Zoe is down.

Big cookie!

Small cookie!

Pink, white, or...

...brown.
(Yum! Yum! Yum!)

Elmo can care.

Zoe can share.

Bert and Ernie say,

"Hello, there!"

# Elmo is sweet.

Oscar is not.

# How much do
# we love you?

This much!

# That's a lot!

# Be sweet!